# Trick

## Sleepover Club

# or Treat

# Jana Hunter

HarperCollins *Children's Books*

The Sleepover Club ® is a registered trademark
of HarperCollins*Publishers* Ltd

First published in Great Britain as *Sleepover Club Witches*
by HarperCollins *Children's Books* in 2002
This edition published by HarperCollins *Children's Books* in 2008
HarperCollins *Children's Books* is a division of HarperCollins*Publishers* Ltd,
77-85 Fulham Palace Road, Hammersmith, London W6 8JB

www.harpercollinschildrensbooks.co.uk

1

Text copyright © Jana Hunter 2002

Original series characters, plotlines and settings © Rose Impey 1997

ISBN-13 978-0-00-727254-9
ISBN-10 0-00-727254-5

Printed and bound in England by
Clays Ltd, St Ives plc

**Mixed Sources**
Product group from well-managed
forests and other controlled sources
www.fsc.org  Cert no. SW-COC-1806
© 1996 Forest Stewardship Council
**FSC**

FSC is a non-profit international organisation established to promote the
responsible management of the world's forests. Products carrying the FSC
label are independently certified to assure consumers that they come
from forests that are managed to meet the social, economic and
ecological needs of present and future generations.

Find out more about HarperCollins and the environment at
**www.harpercollins.co.uk/green**

# The Sleepover Kit List

1. Sleeping bag
2. Pillow
3. Pyjamas or a nightdress
4. Slippers
5. Toothbrush, toothpaste, soap etc
6. Towel
7. Teddy
8. A creepy story
9. Food for a midnight feast: chocolate, crisps, sweets, biscuits. Anything black, red, orange or green!
10. Torch
11. Hairbrush
12. Hair bobble or hairband, if you need them
13. Face paints to make gruesome halloween creatures
14. A change of clothes
15. Sleepover diary and membership card

# 1

Come in, quick. Sit down. I've got something to ask you, and it's dead serious.

Have you got a sister? A crummy big sister? The kind who hates to see you having fun and always tries to ruin things for you? Have you ever wanted to put a spell on that jealous sister? You know, make her disappear, grow warts, or turn into smelly frog-slime and slither off down some deep well? I have, cos my sister Molly really messed up things for the Sleepover Club at Hallowe'en. And it wasn't funny (not at first, anyway). Mind you, when Frankie did her witchy thing and scared everyone half to death it was a killer. The best. And when Rosie went haywire with the Curse of the Nerd's Nose, that was something else.

But that wasn't all.

There was Merlin (my pet rat) and his sneaky trail of rat's droppings. There was the candlelight and the secret chants and all the dark, dark, mysterious goings-on. Then there was the trouble I got into for stealing bits of Molly...

Why she had to make such a fuss about a teeny weeny bit of belly-button fluff, goodness only knows! But that's Molly for you. Always making a big deal. If only she was like my other sister, Emma. Emma's my eldest sister and she's all right, she is. Molly is different. Gruesome. Is it any wonder we call her Molly the Monster?

Look, I know I'm going on about Molly, but she nearly ruined our Sleepover Club, and that's the most important thing in the world to me and my mates, as anyone knows.

Wait. D'you want to hear everything that happened? I bet you do. Okay, here goes... It started on a Friday night. (That's our regular sleepover night, in case you don't know.) It was right before Hallowe'en and the Sleepover Club was getting in the mood for a specially spellbinding time (spellbinding... get it? Spells, potions, witches and stuff). See, my four friends were due at my house any minute. We wanted to work on our trick-or-treat stuff before the dreaded M&Ms, Emma Hughes and Emily Berryman, beat us to it. The M&Ms are our biggest enemies at school and they were sure to have nasty tricks up their sleeves. The gang had some great sleepover things planned: costumes, tricks, witchy games and creepy ghost stories, all topped off with the most wicked midnight feast of black sweets. We had liquorice, Black Jacks, Wine Gums, Fruit Pastilles, jellybeans, Black Imps and best of all, black Jelly Babies! It was going to be the most coo-ell sleepover in history! But of course, Molly the Monster didn't like that. Oh no. She had

9

"Mum promised me," Molly said in that annoying singsong voice she always gets when she thinks she's got one over me. "And anyway Jilly's on her way too... with her mum."

"Too bad the Sleepover Club got in first!" I retorted.

"Too bad for you, Laura McKenzie." Molly made a face at me. But she waited for Mum to leave the kitchen before she gave me one of her big, fat pokes. "Too bad cos I'm having my friend over to stay tonight no matter what. So you can forget your soppy Sleepover Club."

That did it.

How dare she call the Sleepover Club soppy? Our Sleepover Club is the best, the most brilliant fun in the world, and nobody calls it names. For a start it's got me, Kenny, in it (Laura McKenzie to people who want to get on the wrong side of me). But it's also got my best mate Frankie (Francesca Thomas) in it, so that makes it fantabulous, cos Frankie's a real laugh. Then there's Lyndz (Lyndsey Collins) the soft-hearted giggly one, Fliss (Felicity Sidebotham) the sugar-and-spice one and Rosie Cartwright the most down-to-earth grown-up one. We're the five most coo-ell girls in Cuddington School.

And we are not soppy!

That's why when Molly called us that, I had to get my own back by pretending to sigh a huge great sigh. "What a shame there won't be room for your dear little friend to sleep over..." I went. "I s'pose the only thing you can do is camp out in the garage.

'Course, you'll have to share your sleeping bag with Merlin..." Molly hates my rat more than a double dose of poison. "I'm sure Merlin would love to nibble your toes."

That got Molly's back up, big time!

Molly went for me. I went for her. And in no time we were rolling about on the floor like those mad wrestlers you get on telly.

"Ooof!"

"Ouch!"

"Aaargggh!"

It was well good. And I was winning too, when

Mum had to spoil it by coming back into the kitchen.

"Stop it you two! Stop it right now!"

"She started it..."

"You started it!"

"I don't care who started it. Just stop it, or else!"

So because Mum sounded like she meant business this time, my dear sister and I did what she said, although Molly had to carry on making dorky faces at me behind Mum's back.

"Now listen to me," Mum ordered. "I've just been on the phone to Mrs Thomas, and she says since it's an emergency the Sleepover Club can decamp over at Frankie's tonight."

"But everyone's coming here!" I couldn't bear to think of my spider and web decorations upstairs going to waste. "Mum, I've been decorating my room all afternoon."

"I'm sorry, Kenny," said Mum.

"So-rry," mimicked Molly, being her usual super-annoying self. But before I had a chance to thump her, I saw something that would shut her up good and proper.

I saw it loom up out of the dark and float eerily up to the kitchen window, like something out of a horror movie. A sight so gruesome, so horrible, that it sent shivers all the way down to my size three trainers. It was big. It was green. And it had wicked red-rimmed eyes.

"Aaaargh!" screamed Molly, seeing it for herself. "It's a witch!"

"A what?"

"A witch at the window!"

Sure it was a witch. But I wasn't scared. I wasn't shocked. Not me. I just opened my mouth and yelled at the top of my voice:

"Frankie!"

# 2

I raced to the front door, and yanked it open. With the force of a jet-propelled broomstick, the wicked witch herself fell across our hall floor in a heap.

"Come in!" I laughed as the rest of the Sleepover Club tumbled in on top of her. "Oh, I see you already did!"

"Heh, heh, heh..." cackled Frankie-the-witch, looking up at me from the pile of my friends. "Want a bite of my poisoned apple?"

"Save it for Molly," I said. "She deserves it."
I helped Frankie with her pointed hat while the
rest of the Sleepover Club tried to untangle
themselves from the heap of sleeping bags,
sweets, cuddly toys, pillows, bags and Hallowe'en
costumes strewn across the floor.

"You look well ugly!" I told her, dead admiring.

"I know."

"Molly's face!" giggled Lyndz, crawling about
the hall floor, collecting all the scattered
sweets. "She thought it was a real witch come
to cast a spell on her."

"No such thing," said Fliss in her usual
bossy way, as she folded up her sleepover
kit ultra neatly. Fliss is a bit scared of
supernatural things and she tries to cover
it up by acting superior. She's also a total
neatness freak, in case you didn't know.
"Hope you've not squashed my cake, Rosie,"
she fussed.

"Oops." Rosie, who's known for being a bit of
a klutz, went red. "Let me check..."

"Don't bother, Rosie," I told her glumly. "The Sleepover Club's not stopping."

"What!"

"But it's sleepover night!"

"I know. It's over at Frankie's instead."

"Mine?" Frankie's voice sounded muffled behind her green plastic mask. "But we had it at mine last time."

"I know. Molly's messed everything up, as usual."

There were moans of "typical" and "what a Monster". But before we had a chance to think up any worse names for my meddling sister, the doorbell rang and the monster herself flounced out of the kitchen and pushed past me.

"Out the way, little kids," she said, shoving Frankie-the-witch rudely. "I'm having my friend to stay over now. So your baby sleepovers are numbered..."

"Oh yeah?"

"Yeah!"

"What d'you mean?"

Molly looked smug as she delivered her killer

blow. "Jilly's staying here Fridays now. So the Sleepover Club's out!"

We all gaped at her. Then Frankie piped up:

"That's what you think! Our Sleepover Club has rights!" Frankie will always stand up for herself in a fight, especially if she's wearing witch's talons and a pointy hat.

"Rights for you load of babies? You must be joking!" sneered Molly.

"We're not babies!"

"Yes you are!"

"No we're not!"

As you can see, things were getting out of hand, and Total War probably would've broken out if Jilly's mum herself hadn't peeped through the letterbox.

"Hello," she said, in a friendly voice. "Anyone going to let us in?"

This was definitely not the moment to start fighting. So we decided to cool it and plot our revenge over at Frankie's instead.

Because something Had To Be Done.

It's not that we minded sleeping over at Frankie's for the second week running. Frankie's got a huge bedroom with extra bunk beds, so it's well nice having our sleepovers there. (And as Rosie said, a sleepover is a sleepover.) No, we didn't mind so much about staying at Frankie's. It's just that, as Frankie said, "It's the principle of the thing. If Molly starts messing up our sleepovers, who knows what will happen next?"

And the gang agreed.

That's why I did what I did. The horrible, hairy deed itself. I mean, no point in letting a fat, juicy spider go to waste is there?

Carting our stuff through the streets was brilliantly creepy. It was so dark and silent that Frankie-the-witch kept cackling and pretending to put a spell on the houses.

"Eye of newt, toe of bat,
Light of the full moon,

Get lots of sweets for Trick-or-treat...

Cos we are coming soon!"

"Ooo, ooo..." I chanted, waving my hands. "We'll put a spell on you, if you don't!"

But Fliss, whose mum doesn't approve of spells and stuff, was not having any of this. "Why don't we practise our 5ive routine?" she said, ignoring our class act.

"Not now!"

"Why? We've got loads of room out here..."

"NO!"

Course, in the end Lyndz, seeing that Fliss was desperate to get off the scary subject of spells and witches, saved her as usual. Lyndz loves to rescue things. If there was a flea drowning in her tea, she'd probably fish it out and give it the kiss of life. "Come on, you two," she said, doing a 5ive-type kick. "Fliss is right. We've got loads of room to practise our routine here."

So we gave in.

At least, we tried. We tried five times to

dance down the street and sing like our current favourite boy band, but we were so loaded up with stuff it was impossible to do the movements properly. Frankie of course was determined to put some witchy bits into our routine, so she stuffed her rolled-up sleeping bag between her legs and pretended to fly on it down the street. She made us laugh so much our singing went warbly. It was well funny.

Rosie kept dropping things too. She couldn't dance two steps without offloading something. While she was picking up one thing she'd drop two, then three... In the end she just threw everything down in a pile and plonked herself on top. "I give up."

"Me too," said Frankie, unrolling her sleeping bag right there on the pavement as if it was the most normal thing in the world. "It's way past my bedtime." Then, cool as a cucumber, she climbed into her sleeping bag, pulled her pointy hat down to her nose, and pretended to go to sleep.

I told you Frankie was a laugh, didn't I?

Everyone cracked up and poor Lyndz was almost wetting herself. "Oh, stop, stop..." she gasped, clutching her stomach.

"Hey!" Frankie-the-witch stuck her long nose over the edge of her sleeping bag. "Can't a person get some sleep round here?"

That did it. On a silent signal, we unrolled our sleeping bags and laid them out on the pavement, alongside Frankie. All of us except Fliss, Chief Inspector of the Dirt Patrol, that is.

"You'll catch a disease," she predicted darkly.

"Good. Then Molly will be in deep doom forever," I said, pretending to wash my face and brush my teeth before settling down for the night. "It's Molly's fault we've been thrown out on to the streets, anyway. I think we should get the papers to come and take a photo, then she'd really get it."

"Yeah," giggled Lyndz. "I can see the headlines now: "Sleepover Club Is Streets Ahead.""

We laughed, but Fliss was still in a flap, going on about us ruining our clothes. She's the only one in our gang who's into clothes and icky romantic stuff, probably because of her Barbie-doll looks. "Get up, ple-ease," she cried in the end. "I bet dogs have weed on that pavement..."

"Not at this luxury hotel," said Rosie, who was making a night table out of her flattened bag by neatly laying out her hairbrush, headband, toilet bag and diary.

"It's not a hotel."

"'Tis to us."

"Well, I'm not stopping," announced Fliss. "And you'll be sorry if you do!" And with that she grabbed her sleepover kit, and marched off down the street with her nose in the air.

"She'll be back," said Frankie without moving. Actually Frankie hadn't moved since she'd rolled over and pretended to be asleep. "Fliss can't bear to miss a sleepover."

"Maybe she's gone to tell the papers," I offered hopefully.

"Tell her mum, more like."

But Fliss wasn't doing either. In fact, she hadn't gone very far at all.

We went on wondering where she was for a bit, but there's only so much time you can waste worrying at a sleepover. So soon we were telling jokes and sharing black sweets, there on the pavement, as if it was the most normal sleepover in the world. And we got so carried away by our street camp-out that by the time the ghost appeared, Fliss was the last thing on our minds.

"Whhhhoooo-ooooo..."

"Omigosh it's...!"

"Hooo-whhooooo..."

"Quick!"

"Run!"

And in a crazy jumble of sleeping bags, trapped feet and panic, the four of us did the Sack Race of the Century right up to Frankie's front doorstep, screaming loud enough to wake the dead.

Which only goes to prove, you can't keep a Sleepover girl down.

Fliss may be the world's most finicky fusspot but she can still play a wicked ghost when she wants to. Frankie said it was the moans that made her so spooky, but I reckon it was the sleeping bag over the head. You should've heard our screams as we tried to bunny-hop our way over to Frankie's. Reckon the whole of Cuddington did. All the dogs in the neighbourhood went mad, barking and howling, especially Pepsi, Frankie's dog. Frankie's mum said we nearly gave her a heart attack.

Hey, have you ever noticed how screaming makes you starving hungry? It does, you know, because after the Sack Race of the Century everyone was ready for Round Two of the sleepover feast.

Luckily we had masses of stuff.

As well as all the sweets, we had almost-black sausages on sticks, Marmite sandwiches, black grape squash and Fliss's Black Forest cake. We laid everything out in the middle of Frankie's bedroom floor and made a magic circle round the edge of it with her stone collection. It looked dead good. Then we did a little witch dance around it, holding hands and chanting, "Feast, Feast, Feast..."

Pepsi went barmy, especially when Frankie held her paws so she could dance with us on her back legs.

"Ta-daa!" went Rosie. "It's Pepsi the doggie dance star!"

"Woof, woof!"

"Take a bow, Pepsi," said Frankie and Pepsi actually bent her daft black head.

"Woof! Woof, woof!" She loved it.

After that we got down to some serious eating. When we'd demolished the lot, we flopped on the floor, stuffed, and told each other Hallowe'en jokes. They were daft, but they made you laugh. Here are some of my favourites:

**Question:** Why does a witch ride a broomstick?
**Answer:** Because a vacuum cleaner's too heavy.

**Question:** What's a witch's favourite computer programme?
**Answer:** Spellcheck

**Question:** What big, green and smells?
**Answer:** A witch's nose.

Good, aren't they? My very very best, favourite was:

**Lovestruck witch to handsome prince:**
What do I have to give you to make you kiss me?
**Prince:** Chloroform!

That one cracked us all up.

Lyndz laughed so much she got the hiccups. "Hic! What a lovely surprise for the handsome prince when he came round!"

"Talking of surprises…" I said. "That reminds me."

"What?"

"Molly's in for a massive surprise tonight."

"What is it?"

"Tell us!"

I giggled. "A huge hairy spider, hiding in her pyjamas."

"Wicked!"

"Serves her right!"

Frankie put her witch mask back on. (She'd only taken it off so she could eat.) "Heh, heh heh. There came a big spider, that sat down beside her..." she cackled.

"A spider in your pyjamas is so creepy," shuddered Fliss dramatically. "I'd just die!"

"A spider won't stop Molly messing up our sleepovers," Rosie pointed out. Told you Rosie was dead practical and down-to-earth. "We've got to do more than that to stop her."

"Rosie's right. Molly's got swimming practice every Saturday 'til the school gala. We've got to stop her."

"We could snip the straps off her swimming costume," giggled Lyndz, who wouldn't really hurt a fly.

"Or drain the school pool," laughed Rosie.

But Frankie was deadly serious. "Why don't we put a spell on Molly?"

We all stared at her.

"Like what?"

"We could make her so allergic to water she comes out in boils!"

"Er..." I think Frankie was getting a bit carried away with that spooky mask.

"We have to do something, Kenny! Molly's trying to mess up our whole Sleepover Club."

Frankie was right about that, and I could see the others agreed. This was serious. If we didn't put a stop to Molly's tricks the whole club was in danger.

"We-ell..." I said in the end, "I could gatecrash her swimming session tomorrow."

"And do what?"

"Just swim." (Secretly I was hoping to find a way out of putting nasty spells on my sister, even if she did deserve it.) "I'm a better swimmer than Molly and that really makes her mad."

"Hmmm..." said Frankie.

"I can tell her I'll be there every Saturday unless she stops trying to ruin our sleepovers."

"Maybe..."

"They'll let me into the school pool cos I'm Molly's sister."

Frankie thought for a moment longer. "Okay, go to the swimming pool tomorrow... And Kenny?"

"Yeah?"

"Make sure you show Molly who's boss."

"Right."

Next morning I got to Molly's school bright and early.

Outside it was cold and foggy, but inside the pool had that lovely warm, fuggy, chlorine smell. Mind you, I wasn't warm enough to jump in yet. Besides, it was so fogged with steam, I couldn't see Molly at all. So I just stood by the edge, covered in goose pimples, trying to make out one school swimming costume from another.

But that didn't stop Molly the Monster from coming up behind me and making me jump out of my skin. "What are you doing here?" she snarled.

"Mum said I could."

"Liar!" Dripping cold water on to me, Molly stuck her big, wet face into mine. "Mum's already after you for putting that spider in my pyjamas, you little—"

"Oh dear…" I went, all innocent. "Didn't you like my little Hallowe'en surprise, then?"

Molly turned purple. "Get out of here," she hissed. "This is my school pool and my swimming practice."

"You don't own it. I can swim if I want to…" I began.

Molly's face was awful. "Go on then," she snarled. "Swim!"

And she pushed me so hard, I toppled and fell backwards into the pool… splat!

The water hit me across my shoulders like a steel whip and sent shock waves down my body. Down and down I went, gulping and kicking like mad. It was horrible. Horrible and nasty and scary and it seemed to go on forever. It was so bad that when I finally bobbed up, spluttering and gasping for air, I was determined to do one thing.

Beat Molly. As soon as Molly's team was ready for the three-length race, I got into position in an empty lane. No one even noticed me.

They soon would.

**4**

"Laura! Is that you?"

Uh-oh. Mum didn't sound best pleased.

"Can't stop, Mum! I only came to pick up..."

"Laura! Come in here." Even with a mouthful of roller clips Mum could sound fierce. "I want a word with you, my girl."

I poked my head round the kitchen door. Phew! Mum was in the middle of doing a glamorous granny's hair and she'd never tell me off in front of a customer...

Famous last words.

Not only did Mum have a real go at me, but her customer, Mrs Bramley, joined in too. The interfering old granny tut-tutted and nodded 'til every roller on her blue-rinsed head shook.

It was well humiliating.

"Fancy spoiling Molly's swimming practice! I'm surprised at you, Laura. And as for planting a spider in her pyjamas..." Mum went on and on. She used words like 'sneaky' and 'mean' and, worst of all, 'disappointed'. My mum can make 'disappointed' sound the ugliest word in the world.

Then she dropped her bombshell.

"So you can forget sleepovers here."

"WHAT?!"

"Anyone who can wilfully spoil her sister's sleepover doesn't deserve to have her own!" Mum jabbed a roller clip into Mrs Bramley's scalp so hard, the glamorous old granny flinched.

"Ouch!"

"Sorry, Mrs Bramley."

"Mum, you can't stop sleepovers!" I began.

"Oh, can't I?"

"In my day we did what our mothers said..." Mrs Bramley muttered, rubbing her sore head.

"Please, Mu-um! Please, please, pleeease..."

"One more word and I'll get all sleepovers banned," warned Mum. "Molly said it, and the more I think about it, the more I see her point..."

"S-said what?"

"That it's on sleepover nights when the trouble starts."

A cold shiver went through me then. Now I knew what Molly was up to. She was trying to get the Sleepover Club banned for good.

"It's not fair!" I burst out. "Not fair!" And in floods of tears, I raced up to the bathroom and locked myself in for a good cry.

It wasn't fair. How could I explain to Mum that the reason I went to Molly's swimming practice was to stop the gang from casting a spell on her? All my good turns end up with me in trouble. Nobody appreciates me.

I don't know how long I stayed there, sitting on the lid of the toilet, bawling my eyes out. All I know is I used up a whole toilet roll. Then, just as I got to the dry-eyed and puffy-faced stage, I heard something through the bathroom wall. Molly the Monster and Silly Jilly were in the bedroom talking. And Molly sounded worried...

"If goody-goody Robin Hughes has his way, Chess Club will meet Saturday mornings! What'll I do about swimming practice then?"

"Well you can't do both. You're in the Chess Club Tournament."

"I know. Robin Hughes is such a nerd," moaned Molly. "He's sure to get his way."

"Yeah. The teachers love him."

"Like all the Hughes lot. His rotten cousin, Emma, is in my rotten sister's class."

Robin Hughes was one of the dreaded M&Ms' cousins! That was a hot piece of news. But hot or not, Jilly's next words made me go cold.

"Your rotten sister's gonna go ballistic when she finds out about her rat..."

Merlin! My lovely soft, twitchy-nosed pet. What had they done to him? I leapt up and stormed into the bedroom, puffy-faced and panting.

"WHAT HAVE YOU DONE WITH MERLIN!?"

The two conspirators looked up guiltily.

"WELL?"

Molly gave a slow shrug. "We never touched him." But I could tell from the smirky way she slid her eyes over to Jilly that something was up.

In a blind panic, I raced to the garage where I kept Merlin.

Please be all right, Merlin, I prayed. Please be all right.

But the door to my pet's cage was open, and his dear little home was empty.

Merlin was gone.

5

Merlin was gone.

I searched and searched everywhere, but my sweet little pet was nowhere to be found.

Of course, Molly the Monster denied everything. But when Mum questioned Silly Jilly, she couldn't keep it up. The sneaky creep admitted she'd opened the cage just 'to stroke Merlin' (I'll bet!) and that's when he'd shot out.

Molly, you Monster, you were behind this, I fumed to myself.

Jilly would never have gone into the garage if you hadn't told her to cos you're too weedy to touch Merlin yourself. But you planned his escape to get back at me.

That did it.

Determined to pay Molly back, I got on my bike and took off. Fast as a wild witch on a broomstick, I flew down the road to Cuddington library. And I found just what I wanted...

A book on spells.

Back at Frankie's, the rest of the gang was lazing about, watching telly and eating popcorn. They were enjoying the Sleepover Club's usual Saturday treat of swooning over our fave boy bands. Mind you, I could tell Frankie was ready for a distraction.

"OK gang, gather round," I said, spreading *The Good Witches' Guide to Spooky Spells* open on Frankie's bedroom floor. "We've got Hallowe'en to prepare..."

"Wh-what are you going to do?" asked Fliss nervously.

"Learn how to make spells."

"Oh no..."

"Oh, YES!" I declared.

"We won't hurt anybody, Fliss," Lyndz promised.

"All we're doing is reading about spells," said Frankie, leafing through the book. "It's not as if we're going to turn anyone into a toad or anything."

But Fliss wasn't convinced. She went on and on about what her mum would say, and how we'd get into trouble (even though we all knew it was really because she was scared). Fliss can be such a wuss. Just the same, we weren't going to force Fliss to join in. So while we read up about wands and witches' broomsticks, Fliss got busy with an ordinary broomstick and cleaned up our sleepover mess from Frankie's bedroom. (That kept old Fusspot happy!)

What we read was dead interesting. How witchcraft didn't have to be evil, but could be about good magic and making things better. There was even a Good Witches' Code and we all pledged to follow it, to the letter. Learning the right way to do things was really important.

## The Good Witches' Code

1. Do not wish harm on others.
2. Keep matches, oils and candles out of reach from little ones.
3. Get permission to light candles. Never leave candles unattended. Keep lit candles away from curtains, paper etc – anything that may catch fire.
4. Take a friend when out collecting material for spells. Don't go anywhere dangerous and let a responsible adult know where you plan to go.
5. Don't do any spell that means getting into a bath when you're tired. You might fall asleep!
6. Know your plants – which are poisonous,

and which are endangered species – before you pick them.

7. Do not apply essential oils directly to the skin, without proper dilution.

8. Never drink or eat any of the ingredients to any spell.

9. Do not wear floaty sleeves or trailing clothes for casting spells, in case of accident.

10. Whatever you attempt, GET PERMISSION FIRST!

We were so engrossed in spells and shells, potions, lotions and charms, that I almost forgot my troubles.

Almost.

Merlin and the danger the Sleepover Club was in bubbled away inside me like a witch's cauldron. Bubble, bubble, bubble.

"Fliss, you'd like this one," said Lyndz, pointing to Fairy Luck. "You make a magic wreath of ferns and ivy sprayed with rosewater and hang it on your front door."

"If you want fairies to come," scoffed Frankie.

"I think it's sweet," Fliss sighed in spite of herself. "Getting all the little fairies to dance around at the bottom of your garden." Then she did a little ballet dance just to prove it.

Frankie gave a snort of laughter. She quoted from Peter Pan, "If you believe in fairies, just clap your hands!"

We all clapped like mad just for a laugh. Then Frankie did a wicked imitation of Peter Pan whooping and flying across the sky, I mean room. So me and Lyndz did a Native American war dance on the beds while Rosie pretended to be Captain Hook. (Guess who had to be Tinkerbell?)

We had an ace pillow fight between the Native Americans and the pirates, then we went back to our spellbook.

When we got to the section on spells for Harmony in the Home, Rosie got thoughtful. "I'd really like to cast one of these spells," she said, all wistful and sad. "My house is such a tip."

Rosie's home was a bit of a mess. Her dad's in

the building trade and when he split up with her mum, he left the house like a builders' yard.

"I think these spells are about harmony in the family. Not DIY," I pointed out gently.

"We could do with family harmony too," sighed Rosie.

I reckon Rosie hoped her dad would come back home and the family would be happy together again (even though her mum's got a new boyfriend). Personally, I think Rosie-Posie was dreaming.

"I'm going to do a spell for Pepsi to have pups," said Frankie, who was desperate for more pets. "There's one here for babies, so I don't see why it can't work for dogs."

"Shame you won't need a brother or sister any more," I said. "You could've had my sister anytime."

Frankie pulled a face. "No thanks!"

We all laughed. Frankie's an only child, but not for much longer! She used to moan about being an only child, but now her mum's expecting a baby, all Frankie's dreams are coming true.

"What about you, Fliss?"

"We-ell, I would make a spell for this wonderful outfit I've seen in Designer Fashions but..." Fliss, who had turned her favourite colour of pink, trailed off.

"I'm going do a horse spell!" announced Lyndz. "For a horse of my own."

Frankie's reply rhymed: "A horse, of course!" She gave a loud neigh, "Neeeeeeigh..." and pawed the air.

We all fell about laughing, so Lyndz got up and did a noisy gallop round the room, jumping over our sprawled out bodies as if we were fences. Naturally Frankie had to raise the stakes by sticking her bottom in the air even higher.

"And it's Lyndsey Collins on Merrylegs, coming up to the final fence," Lyndz announced, pretending to rear at the sight of Frankie's bottom stuck up in the air.

Suddenly 'Merrylegs' threw back her head, snorted and took a running gallop at Frankie.

"YES!!!" we cheered as she sailed through the air.

"Neeeeeeigh!" 'Merrylegs' whinnied as she bashed into Frankie's bum.

"Watch out for the other riders!" I yelled.

"Aaargh!" We ended up in a heap in the middle of the room, rolling about and kicking like stallions.

It was well funny. But it couldn't make me forget that Merlin was still missing. It couldn't stop me worrying about him, and it couldn't stop me thinking about what I had to do.

"I'm gonna put a spell on Molly the Monster," I announced at last.

"Yay!" cheered Frankie.

"You can't wish hurt on another," Fusspot Fliss reminded me.

"Who said I would?" I mumbled rather feebly.

"Fliss, we have to stop Molly from ruining our sleepovers," said Frankie. "What kind of a spell are you going to put on her, Kenny?"

"A Love Potion."

"A Love Potion?!" My mates all gawped.

"Yeah," I grinned. "For my dear sister Molly to fancy someone like mad."

Fliss, the one who loves lurrve so much she even marries her toys, was dead excited. "Who? Who will Molly fancy?"

"Are you sure you want to know?" I teased her.

Fliss thwacked me. And she was so keen to know my secret, she even forgot to be afraid of spells.

"Emma Hughes' cousin," I said. "Robin Hughes, the nerd."

Payback time! Just you wait, Molly McKenzie!

In order to make a spell for Molly, I had to gather as many bits of her as possible. Altogether I needed:

1.  Nail clippings
2.  Strand of hair
3.  A shred of fluff
4.  Red wax candle
5.  Nail (the other kind of nail)

6. A teaspoon of rainwater
7. A fingerprint from subject's 'love object'

With a bit of know-how, it wouldn't be too hard to get a nail clipping or a hair or two. Trouble was, how was I supposed to get a fingerprint from Molly's 'love object'?

There had to be a way.

I thought and thought about it the whole of Sunday. I thought about it as I searched and searched for Merlin (and didn't find him). I thought about it as I scarfed down roast beef, Yorkshire pudding and a double helping of apple crumble. And I thought about it in bed. But, all I could think of was kidnapping Robin Hughes, and I didn't fancy that. I mean, what would we do with him, when we got him?

Then, just as I was about to fall asleep, it came to me! An idea so coo-ell, so ace and top, I nearly jumped out of bed.

At school on Monday, I told Frankie about my brainwave.

"Brillo!" Frankie gave me a high five. "Kenny, you're a star."

"You said it," I beamed. Frankie catches on quickly.

At break the two of us put the first part of the 'Love Potion Plan' into action. It relied on the M&Ms' love of meddling, so no problem there! But it also meant following the horrible pair, known as the Goblin and the Queen, into the girls' toilets at break. (The things we do for the Sleepover Club!)

We waited until the M&Ms were safely locked in the two end toilets. Then all we had to do was pretend to be having a private little chat, so that our enemies could accidentally-on-purpose overhear us.

"Frankie..." I began in an extra loud whisper.

"Yes, Kenny?" hissed Frankie.

"You know, Robin Hughes is gonna die if he hears my sister Molly fancies him!"

Frankie stifled a laugh. "Yeah. Robin mustn't ever find out that Molly's mad for him!"

"Exactly." I gave Frankie a huge wink. "It would ruin things Big Time for the Sleepover Club, if those two got together."

Stage One done. Cool as cucumbers, Frankie and I sauntered out of the girls' toilets. It didn't take long. We knew our trick had worked when the M&Ms went into one of their major heads-together whisperings in the corner of the playground. Those two love the chance to ruin things for the Sleepover Club.

And just to prove it, they did something only the M&Ms could do. It was in Arts & Crafts. Our class was doing Hallowe'en collages to decorate the classroom walls. We had orange and black paper, beads, fabric scraps, lots of autumn leaves, acorns and stuff and gallons of glue. Everyone was busily cutting and sticking, when suddenly Frankie burst out, "Wow! Just what I need for my spell for Pepsi's pups!"

"What?"

"Pearls!" Frankie pounced on an old string of fake pearls, which were tangled up with the ribbons and yarn. "The Baby Spell calls for pearls..."

Baby Spell!

Emma Hughes' eyes nearly popped out her head. Wow! Did she and her stupid partner go into a major heads-together thing this time! But it wasn't until clean-up time that we found out what they'd been up to. We were in the middle of cleaning up when Mrs Weaver said sternly, "Francesca Thomas, come out here."

The Goblin shot a look of triumph at the Queen. Frankie got up slowly and went over to Mrs Weaver's desk. "Yes, Miss?"

"I hope you haven't been stealing school property, Francesca," Mrs Weaver said severely. "You know how wrong that is."

Frankie flushed. "Yes, Miss... I mean, no Miss. I..."

"Have you taken something, Francesca?"

The class went dead silent. So silent you could probably hear my heart thumping in the stillness! But Frankie didn't answer.

Suddenly Mrs Weaver's voice cut through the silence. "Francesca," she ordered. "EMPTY YOUR POCKETS!"

Lyndz whimpered. Rosie clasped her hands. And Frankie turned all colours of the sun. My best friend hung down her head, then started to empty her pockets. One by one, she took out her secret private stuff:

One squirrel with a chipped tail (from miniature ornament collection)
One silver moon earring
One half-eaten packet of bubble gum
One used paper hankie
One dog biscuit with crumbs
A bit of pocket fluff
One 2p piece
A scrap of pink ribbon

Everyone craned their necks to inspect the evidence.

"I–I just took this ribbon from the bin, Miss..." Miserably, Frankie held up the crumpled scrap of pink ribbon. "Someone had thrown it away, so I thought it was OK..."

Mrs Weaver coughed. "Oh. Oh, I see."

Another long silence.

"Miss, are these what you're looking for, Miss?" I said finally, holding up the pearls that Frankie had put back in the collage box.

The M&Ms gasped.

Frankie threw me a grateful smile and Mrs Weaver turned the same colour as Frankie's ribbon.

"Oh! Oh, yes. Thank you, Laura." Then smiling ever-so sweetly at Frankie, Mrs Weaver said, "All right, Francesca, you can sit down now."

Whew! Frankie was innocent. Nobody but the M&Ms could ever have thought different.

Even so, it didn't stop Frankie from feeling just awful.

"It was as if I'd committed the major crime of the century," she shuddered. "Standing up there, in front of the whole class..."

"But you hadn't done anything," Lyndz comforted her. "And Mrs Weaver knew it."

"Those M&Ms..." muttered Rosie, shaking her head. "When will their meddling stop?"

"Not yet, I hope!" I snorted.

"Why? What d'you mean, Kenny?" asked Rosie, puzzled.

"If I get my way, the M&Ms' meddling is going to help save the Sleepover Club!"

"Huh?"

"Tell us, tell us!" begged Lyndz.

I looked at Frankie. She looked at me. "Tell them Kenny! Tell them!"

So we let the gang into our plan. How Frankie and I made sure the M&Ms overheard us. And how they were bound to set up Robin Hughes with Molly, just to foil us.

"Once Molly thinks someone likes her, it won't matter whether she thinks he's the biggest nerd in the world, the flattery will go to her head. She's sure to choose Chess Club to be near

Robin Hughes," I finished.

"I know Robin Hughes," announced Fliss importantly. "He lives round the corner."

"That could come in very useful," I said thoughtfully.

"But how will Molly fancying Robin Hughes help the Sleepover Club?" persisted Rosie, who could be a bit slow on the uptake sometimes.

"Well, if she's not going to swimming on Saturdays any more she won't need Silly Jilly to sleep over."

"So...?"

"So that means she won't need to get our sleepovers stopped."

"She'll be too busy with her new boyfriend to worry about ruining our club," explained Frankie.

"Excellent!" cheered Lyndz and Fliss.

"Brillo!" Rosie had to agree.

I huffed on my fingertips and rubbed them on my school sweatshirt. "Thank you, gang. How clever of you to notice!"

Now all we had to do was wait. The M&Ms

would take care of the next bit for us, for sure.

Thank you, M&Ms... Thank you for helping us save our Sleepover Club!

# 7

Fliss was in heaven. "Ooh, look at these!" she sighed. "And these, and these!"

It was half term and we were in Harmony Heaven getting all the stuff for our spells. There were lotions and potions, mirrors, silver trinkets and tinkly glass wind chimes everywhere. The place was like Aladdin's Cave.

Rosie was sorting through the same basket of shells Fliss was sighing over. "You can almost see through this one," she said.

"Ooh! Perfumed candles!" gushed Fliss, rushing over to a glass shelf loaded with goodies.

Frankie rolled her eyes. "How romantic!"

Ignoring Frankie's teasing, Fliss was now going mad on all the smelly stuff. "My mum would love these!" she said as she sniffed a packet of bath salts. "She says you should always take care of yourself and find time to wind down."

Just as I was thinking that Fliss's houseproud mum needed more than bath salts to make her relax, Lyndz ran up. "Look!" she said excitedly. "A bottle of coloured sand. My spell says that all I have do is sprinkle sand on the ground, and write 'Merrylegs' in it!"

"What for?"

Lyndz thwacked Frankie. "To get my dream horse, Donkey Brain!"

"Neeeeigh!" whinnied Frankie, remembering our last horsey game.

"Brrrrr!" Lyndz snorted back, and she reared just like a horse.

"Go for it, Merrylegs!" I cheered and Lyndz

pawed the ground. But when she pretended to write 'Merrylegs' with her 'hoof', she knocked over a basket of novelty sponges and a plaster mermaid.

We scrabbled on the floor, collecting seahorse and fish-shaped sponges, in total hysterics. But our laughter died a sudden death as the shopkeeper marched over. "Are you girls planning on making a purchase?" she demanded, waving her jangly bracelets in the air.

"Er..."

"We were..."

"We were just horsing around," Frankie finished, and before I could stop it, a snort of laughter had escaped from behind my hand.

The shopkeeper swelled up. "Young lady, if you're going to be rude..."

"Sorry," I cut in. "We're really sorry. And... and I do want to buy something." I stroked a red candle against my cheek. "I'd like this for my... Lu-u-rve Potion."

Uh-oh. Everyone got the giggles big time

now. The only one who didn't find it amusing was you-know-who.

Shopkeepers hate kids.

So, after we bought what we needed for our spells, we agreed to boycott her stupid shop just to show her.

We did much better collecting pebbles in the White Swan pub's driveway. The man who owned the place was dead friendly. "Make a wish for me," he grinned. "To win the Lottery!"

"No problem!"

Things were going great. We had our candles, our shells, our sand and our pebbles. Now all we had to do was go to the Arboretum to collect twigs for wands.

The Arboretum is this huge tree park smack bang in the middle of Leicester. It's peaceful and green and has every kind of tree you can think of. We had no trouble finding the ones s'posed to have magical powers, hazel and rowan.

"Look at this." I rubbed the grey bark of a hazel tree. "You can tell it's magic."

"Only take twigs from the ground," cut in Frankie just as I was trying out a magic chant. Frankie collected signatures with her mum for 'Save a Tree' once and it's made her a bit bossy about living things.

"We care about the environment too, you know," I protested.

But my promise didn't stop Fliss the-ever-nervous-one from going, "Watch out no one sees us."

"We're not doing any harm," Lyndz consoled her.

"Heh, heh, heh!" I gave a wicked witch cackle. "That's what you think!" And waving my hazel wand about, I chanted:

"Eye of newt, slimy toad stew...
Time to put a spell on you!"

Cackling evilly, I chased the gang round the Arboretum threatening to turn them into frogs. It was well funny.

The gang went mad, and Frankie went

haywire as usual. She raced round the trees and slid on her bum down the grass slopes yelling, "A witch! A witch!" Rosie nearly wet herself.

We were all shrieking and running like wild things, when suddenly Fliss stopped dead in her tracks.

"L-look over there," she panted, pointing to a boy the other side of the grass.

"Where?" We looked.

"It's Robin Hughes!" Fliss gasped.

We all looked at a tall skinny boy standing under a tree taking notes.

"So that's my future brother-in-law!" I joked.

"Only if your spell works," laughed Frankie.

Robin Hughes, who was more like Harry Potter than Harry Potter himself, looked up from his notepad and blinked at us through his glasses.

"Robin!" shouted out Fliss. "This is Molly's sister. She's got a message for you!"

The poor boy went white.

"You know, Molly who's in the chess tournament?" I added.

"D-do you mean M-Molly M-McKenzie?" Robin stuttered.

"Yeah," I said as I ran up to him. "Hasn't your cousin Emma told you about her?"

"Well... yes, actually," said Robin, looking dead embarrassed.

"My sister says she wants to know when it's Chess Club. She really wants it to be Saturday."

"Oh," said Robin looking relieved. "Tell her it's going to be on Saturdays then."

Now it was my turn to feel relieved. If Chess Club was on Saturdays, the Sleepover Club might be out of danger!

But just to make sure I said, "Molly really wants to see you."

Robin went red. "Really...?"

There was an awkward silence. Then Robin seemed to screw up all his courage. In a sudden rush, he blurted out, "Tell her I'll see her there!"

(YES!)

"OK."

"See ya, Robin!"

"R-right."

Heh, heh, heh... Our little plot was working.

# 8

"Let me clean the bath, Mum!" I grabbed the Ajax and Mum's jaw dropped a mile.

"Thank you, Kenny," she said, trying to act like it was the most normal thing in the world for me to offer to clean the bath after Molly the Monster. (I don't think so!)

Mind you, Mum wasn't the only one surprised at me lately. Believe it or not, in the last two days, I had sorted laundry, tidied Molly's side of the bedside table (even though Molly throws away anything of mine that goes on to her side) and cleaned her yucky hairbrush.

How else was I supposed to collect bits of Molly's horrible grunge for my witchy spell? But even a magical person has limits. When I had to fish out a bit of her horrible toenail from the bath, I almost threw up.

Molly the Monster had taken to having long, private baths ever since I gave her Robin's message about Chess Club. She didn't fancy him (yet!) but even a nerd showing interest in you is better than no one. So with Saturday looming, my gruesome sister was probably trying to decide which club she'd go to – swimming or chess. The suspense was killing me!

But that wasn't the only thing looming. Hallowe'en was next week. The thing was, we'd got fab stuff planned for our Hallowe'en sleepover, but so far we had nowhere to have it.

Every parent had said a big fat "No".

See, the ugly rumour that our Sleepover Club was 'trouble' had spread. Jilly's mum was friendly with Lyndz's mum and the two of them had a real downer on us (all Silly Jilly's doing, of course). They were forever on the phone, complaining about things the gang got up to at sleepovers. And as soon as the other mums got wind of this, they started being mardy about sleepovers too.

True, with all my cleaning, my mum was definitely softening… But there was no way she'd go back on her word to ban sleepovers at our house. Not yet, anyway. When even Mrs Thomas gave a weak excuse, things looked desperate.

So the Sleepover Club had a conference call.

A conference call is where phone lines are linked up so different people can speak together at the same time. Here's how it works with our gang.

We've all got mobiles now, amazingly. First, I call Frankie on our home phone. Next, Frankie answers me and calls Lyndz on her mobile. Then Lyndz answers on her home phone and calls Fliss on her mobile. Fliss answers on her mobile

worked. "This is going to be the best Hallowe'en ever!" I cheered.

But Fliss was not so enthusiastic. "A sleepover in the McKenzie caravan!" she shivered. "It's probably full of spiders!"

"We can use them for Hallowe'en," Frankie teased.

"I'm not sleeping there!" insisted Fliss.

"Well we can't have our sleepover at your house," I retorted. "Your mum hates the mess!"

Fliss had to admit this was true.

"Mine's out too," Frankie reminded us. "My mum and dad are going to a Hallowe'en party and they said our gang's too much for any babysitter."

"My mum's gone all weird about the Sleepover Club ever since she bumped into Jilly's mum," said Lyndz. "But Kenny? Isn't the caravan haunted?"

"Don't!" whispered Fliss.

"Not any more," I said. "We went camping in it last summer and had a great time."

"Well, I think it's perfect for our Hallowe'en spells," said Rosie, who still preferred not to have sleepovers at her house.

And that decided it.

Our Hallowe'en sleepover was going to be in the famous McKenzie caravan.

Personally, I couldn't wait.

"Frankie, can you pin on my wings?" I asked.

"Wait 'til I finish sticking on my witch's talons," came Frankie's muffled voice from behind her witch mask.

"I'll do it," offered Lyndz, ever helpful. Though she made the whole caravan shake as she clumped over in her riding boots.

"Woof, woof!"

"Pepsi, stop rocking the boat!" Pepsi was jumping about like a mad thing, and making the caravan rock even more.

"Woof, woof!"

Yes, you guessed it! We were in the caravan dressing up in our Hallowe'en costumes.

Hallowe'en at last!

Everyone had got fantastic costumes. Fliss was a fairy in a pink (natch!) tutu from her ballet class. Her mum had curled her blonde hair into ringlets and she even had a sparkly tiara on top. She looked dead good. Rosie was a white witch (that means she was a good one) in one of her mum's nighties and Lyndz was a jockey in jodhpurs and riding hat. Frankie, as you know, was the famous wicked witch who had scared Molly before…

And me? Well, I was Cupid the love cherub who was going to shoot my lurrrrrrve arrow straight into the heart of Molly and Robin. Unfortunately the arrows were only rubber tipped! Though I say it myself, I looked fab with my curly clown's wig and tissue paper wings. I'd even got a plastic bow and arrow from an old Robin Hood costume. Mind you,

Frankie reckoned if I really wanted to look like Cupid, I should go starkers!

Thank goodness Rosie pointed out I'd freeze my bum off in this weather!

October in Leicester is not the best time for running round in skimpy costumes. That's why our mums made us promise to wear our school coats between houses when we went trick-or-treating. But nothing was gonna stop our gang having a wicked Hallowe'en.

Mind you, Frankie was not keen on doing trick-or-treat at all at first. She reckoned we were too old for all that baby stuff. But Lyndz, who wouldn't miss out on the chance for sweets, won her over. She said it'd be cool if we only went to friends' and neighbours' houses.

"Does Robin Hughes count?" I asked, aiming an arrow at his imaginary heart.

"'Course," said Fliss, waving her sparkly wand about. "He's my neighbour, isn't he?"

Fliss was right. And luckily that made my plan to save the Sleepover Club easier.

Soon all our troubles would be over. Molly would give up swimming and go to Chess Club, Mum's ban would be over and Silly Jilly would never have to sleep over at our house again!

We had our spell-making Hallowe'en Sleepover all planned out.

1. Dress up in caravan
2. Trick-or-treat
3. Get Robin Hughes' fingerprint
4. Cast spells
5. Eat Hallowe'en sweets
6. Tell ghost stories
7. Eat more sweets
8. Stay up
9. Eat loads more sweets!
10. Oh yes, and go to sleep some time

By 7.30pm, we'd nearly finished number two of our list. We'd visited our houses and our neighbours' houses and got a ton of goodies. Our bags were bursting!

Fliss's street was the last to go...

"Thanks, Mrs Sidebotham!"

"Happy Hallowe'en!"

Outside the gate, we slipped our coats back on, swapped sweets and wondered whether to knock on the Grumpies' door. The Grumpies are Fliss's snooty neighbours, the Watson-Wades, and they didn't get their nickname for nothing! They're so fussy about their posh house, our gang's always getting into trouble with them.

"It's no good asking them for sweets," Fliss sighed, probably remembering the earwigging she got from her mum over the Grumpies. "Mrs Watson-Wade says sweets are nasty sticky things and she wouldn't have them in her house."

"So…" Frankie was sucking on a ginormous gobstopper, "we should play a trick on them!"

"Like what?"

"T.P. their house."

"What's that?" asked Rosie, unwrapping another treacle toffee.

"T.P. stands for toilet paper," said Frankie with a grin.

"And it means we wrap their house in toilet paper. The roof, the tree, everything," I added.

"Don't be daft, Kenny!" said Rosie with her mouth full. "How could we climb…?"

But she didn't have time to finish, because Frankie-the-witch was already creeping up the Grumpies' driveway.

NEENAH! NEENAH!

Suddenly alarm bells went off and lights floodlit the garden. Dogs barked and the whole place was lit up like a prison camp in one of those old war films. The door to the Grumpies' house was flung open and Mrs Watson-Wade, with a face like a gruesome zombie, appeared.

"SCARPER!" hissed Frankie, so the five of us legged it down the driveway and up the street. And before Mr Watson-Wade had time to shout, "Pack of wild animals!" we had disappeared round the corner.

"That was close!" panted Frankie.

"I'm not going back there," Fliss said breathlessly.

Me neither. We had enough to do without getting arrested by the Grumpies for disturbing the peace. For a start, we needed to collect a fingerprint from Robin Hughes.

Holding on to my side, I panted, "Fliss, have you got the cupcakes for Robin?"

Fliss nodded and opened a tin of scrummy chocolate cupcakes. Yum, yum! Mrs Sidebotham may be strict about keeping her kitchen clean, but she is an ace cook! Little did she know how her cooking was going to help save the Sleepover Club...

The Hughes' house didn't have any burglar alarms, but the nerd himself still looked surprised to see us.

"Hello, Robin," said Fliss, putting on her soppy 'fairy' voice.

Robin was too interested in Frankie's mask to notice Fliss's fairy outfit. "We don't have any sweets," he said, staring at the mask. "My mum doesn't believe in sugar."

"You can have some of ours…" Fliss opened the tin of cupcakes. "Your mum won't mind these, cos they're homemade."

"Thanks!" Robin licked his lips. Then he picked the biggest cupcake and took such a huge bite he got chocolate all over his big nose.

Frankie snorted behind her mask and Lyndz started to giggle. But it gave me a perfect chance. "Wait!" I grabbed the cake.

"Hey!" protested Robin.

"Er… sorry. That's the one the dog licked," I lied. I put the cupcake very carefully back in the tin. "Have another one instead."

Robin looked puzzled but he scoffed another cupcake anyway. (Some boys may be clever, but girls can still get one over them.)

"Molly sent her love to you," was my parting shot to the Chess Wiz. And underneath the globs of chocolate his face turned pink.

"What are you going to do with that cake Robin started?" asked Rosie as we turned the corner.

"Mix it in the Love Potion, of course."

"Why?" Rosie can be so dim sometimes.

"Because it has his thumb print on it, Lame Brain!"

"Ohhhh. Clever."

"You said it!" My plan was going so well that I almost danced down the street.

Lyndz started to giggle. "What about when Robin got chocolate all over his nose?"

"I think some even went up it."

"Eeeuw." Fliss made out she was being sick.

"That cake's probably got his snot all over it!"

"Or a big bogey…"

"What a nerd."

We fell about the pavement, killing ourselves. "What a nerdy nerd nerd!"

That's when Rosie went haywire. She started waving her arms about, shouting, "The Curse of the Nerd's Nose! The Curse of the Nerd's Nose!" and chased us down the street.

The five of us raced, yelling like mad, all through the dark streets of Cuddington… and all the way back to the caravan.

The caravan looked magic in the candlelight. Mum had given us candle holders and shown me where it was safe to stand them, and we had draped fake spider webs everywhere. We'd stuck glow-in-the-dark pumpkins and ghosts all over the walls and Lyndz had tied a magic wreath to the caravan's door handle. She'd made it with straw from the stables and ivy from her back garden.

"It will bring us fairy luck," she said, and Fliss did a little bit of fairy ballet, just to be sure.

"Fliss, you're s'posed to say:

"Come in from the mist of silvery dew,
Come gather dance and play,
Pixies, elves and fairies too
Come to us today,"

Lyndz chanted.

"I did already. I said it on my own in my

garden." Fliss was still nervous about doing spells.

Not me. I think Hallowe'en is coo-ell!

So does Frankie. She loved all the mystery and witchcraft and she wanted to do a Broomstick Incantation before we got started on our spells, to make the caravan more magical. So we sat in a magic circle on the floor and watched while she got herself into a witchy mood. Frankie's blue plastic kitchen broom didn't look much like a witch's broomstick, but as Rosie said, "a broom is a broom".

"Now for my incantation," Frankie muttered, dead creepy-like.

"Uh-oh."

"Sshh!" hissed Frankie as Lyndz started giggling.

"Sorry." Lyndz clapped her hand over her mouth so hard she got the hiccups. "Hic! Hic!"

Uh-oh. Once Lyndsey Collins gets the hiccups, that's it. We tried scaring her and making her hold her breath, but it was no good. In the end, Frankie said she we'd have to ignore her or we'd be here 'til next Hallowe'en.

So apart from the occasional 'hic', everything went quiet. In the eerie candlelight Frankie tied a green ribbon on her broom handle. Then she tied a yellow one next to it. Dead tricky with witch's talons glued to your fingernails, so it took an extra long time.

"Pretty!" said Fairy Fliss when it was done. And she tapped the broom with her sparkly wand.

"The yellow ribbon's s'posed to be gold," Frankie explained, "but I couldn't find any. Ooops! I forgot, I'm supposed to say something while I'm tying the ribbons!" So Frankie had to untie the ribbons and start all over again. This time she chanted:

"This caravan is filled with magic,
And this broom is my lucky charm."

It made you shiver. Especially when Frankie

closed her eyes and walked round our magic circle with the broom stuck out in front of her.

"What are you doing now?" Rosie wanted to know.

"Sweeping away unwanted energy… Clearing away for the new…" Frankie whispered in a strange voice.

"Ouch!"

"Sorry," said Frankie who'd stepped on Lyndsey's hand.

"Hic!"

Frankie sighed and closed her eyes to concentrate. Then she turned round and round on the spot, sweeping around herself in one big circle, and chanting:

"Here I sweep,
Round and round,
Drawing a magic circle
On the ground."

We were all getting totally spooked when

Frankie snapped open her eyes and announced in her normal voice, "That's it."

We all jumped.

"It's dead magical in here now!"

"Coo-ell!"

It did feel magic. Our gang is so good at Pretend you end up believing it.

Next it was Lyndsey's turn for her Merrylegs spell. She had all the stuff for it, but the trouble is, Lyndz can't be serious about anything. When she started pawing in the sprinkled sand, she hiccuped so much she got the giggles big time. So we all made horsey noises to help her along.

"Neeeeeigh…"

Dunno if spells work when you're mucking about, but Lyndz was ever hopeful. "Now all I have to do is wait for my horse."

"How long?" Rosie looked round the caravan as if expecting the horse to gallop in any minute.

"Dunno," said Lyndz.

Rosie had already done her spell, so she

didn't need to do any more. She'd had to thread shells and bells on to two long bits of thread and hang one each outside her own house and her dad's. "It's s'posed to help bring peace and harmony in divorced homes," she explained.

Nobody said anything. We knew how much this meant to Rosie and we hoped, for her sake, it worked.

Next it was Frankie's turn to do Pepsi's Puppy Spell. Pepsi was dead good when Frankie tied bits of pink and blue wool to her tail, and she wagged it like mad when it was finished. But when it came to turning three times in the middle of the circle, the daft dog was hopeless. She thought it was a game and kept trying to jump on to Frankie's lap.

"Stay, Pepsi! Stay!"

Pepsi sat down obediently and wagged her decorated tail.

"Now turn around. Turn around, Pepsi."

Pepsi leapt up and lunged at Frankie, bowling

her over and licking her witch's mask.

"Woof, woof!"

"Pepsi, you're never going to have puppies at this rate," Frankie-the-witch laughed.

And the Sleepover gang had to agree.

At last. Time for my Love Spell.

A thrill went right through me.

While the rest of the gang chanted "Robin, Molly, Robin, Molly," I mixed my powerful Love Potion in a plastic beaker:

1.  One toenail (Molly's)
2.  Scrap of belly button fluff
3.  Crumb of toe jam
4.  One long hair

5. One half-eaten cupcake with thumbprint
6. Teaspoon of rainwater to moisten

I did a bit of swaying with my eyes closed, to make it more real, and muttered witchy-type things. I don't know how long I was supposed to do it, but when the potion felt all gloppy and mixed, I set it carefully in the middle of the circle.

Rosie inspected it. "This'd be a wicked mixture for a Sleepover dare." (Rosie was probably remembering the time she had to eat 'Nappy's Brains' to get into the Sleepover Club.)

"Yuck!"

"Sssh!" I scratched the initials 'R' and 'M' either end of the red candle I'd got in Harmony Heaven. Then I broke the candle in half and rubbed the two bits of it together, just for good luck.

"Ahhh, it's like they're kissing…" sighed Fliss.

"We have to do the next part outside," I said.

"Why?"

"My mum said we weren't to play with candles in the caravan."

There was a bit of grumbling about the cold, but in the end, we all put on our school coats and trooped out into the dark.

"Get into a circle again," I commanded.

They all huddled together, looking very unmagical.

"It's cold!" Fliss complained.

Honestly. "Are we doing this or not?" I huffed.

So the gang formed a disgruntled circle.

I lit the two pieces of candle. Then, slowly, slowly I began dripping wax from each burning piece into the Love Potion. The melted wax sizzled and turned into red blobs the second it hit the potion.

"Cool! Looks like drops of blood."

"Eeuch!"

Ignoring them, I went on dripping. Drip, drip, stir and chant. Drip, drip, stir and chant:

"Come Robin, come to Molly.
You know why, but can't deny
Your need to come to Molly.

"Come Molly, come to Robin.
You know why, but can't deny
Your need to come to Robin."

Everything felt suddenly real, especially when the moon went behind a cloud. It was very cold and very very dark.

Fliss shivered. "Feels like we're being watched. Let's go back inside."

Was it the moon, or the wind whispering in the bushes? But I felt it too and so did the others. Without another word, we stumbled back up the caravan steps. Fast.

Inside the caravan, I set the potion in the middle of the circle. Then I chanted the extra bit I'd made up, just to save our Sleepover Club:

"Molly and Robin, Robin and Molly,
Meet at Chess Club on Saturdays.
Leave our Sleepover Club alone,
And stop your sneaky ways!"

Suddenly there was a low ghostly moan, and the caravan began to shake.

"Wh-what's that?" Fliss quavered.

Softly at first, the caravan shook, then more and more, until the whole thing was swaying like a boat out at sea. Pepsi whimpered, Fliss screamed and Lyndz's hiccups disappeared.

The moaning went on… Then along the sides of the caravan was a scrabbling sound, scrabble, scrabble, scrabble, as if hundreds and thousands of long bony fingers were clawing to get in.

"Wh-what is it?"

We were too terrified to do anything but cling together for dear life, trembling like mad. And the moaning was getting louder.

After the longest two minutes in our whole

lives, Lyndz had a brainwave. "F-Fliss, call my brother!" she whispered.

"H-how?"

"On your mobile!"

Fliss usually had her mobile with her the whole time. But her fairy costume had nowhere to keep her mobile, so we were out of luck.

"I want my mum!" cried Fliss.

"Frankie, you and Kenny run to the house!" said Rosie.

"No way," Frankie trembled.

"Send Pepsi with a note, then."

But Pepsi was cowering against Frankie's leg. She was going nowhere.

We couldn't go out and we couldn't stay there.

What could we do?

Hide? Faint? Die of fright? Probably. We'd be found years later, five frozen girls and a spaniel with bows on her tail.

There was only one thing left to do.

Together we took deep breaths and opened our mouths. In one long shriek we screamed louder and longer than we've ever screamed before. We screamed and screamed and screamed, until it felt like we'd never ever stop.

"Aaaaaaaaaaaaargh!"

And that's when slowly, very slowly, the door to the caravan creaked open.

# 11

"DAD!"

Mega-relieved, I flung myself at my dad, and held on to him tight.

But Dad wasn't feeling so loving. "What in heaven's name is going on here!" he yelled.

Everyone tried to answer, but their voices were drowned by my dad's yelling. Dad's explosions don't come often, but when they do – watch out! He shouted that he could hear our screaming all the way from the back bedroom.

And just in case he couldn't, the next-door neighbours had phoned to tell him all about it. "You've probably woken half the neighbourhood!" Dad hollered in a voice loud enough to wake the other half.

"Sorry..."

"I don't know what you think you're playing at…"

"Just having a bit of Hallowe'en fun, Dad..."

"Hallowe'en or not, you blah, blah, blah..."

Dad went on and on.

I thought he'd never stop.

Only good thing was, Molly and Jilly got it in the neck even more than the Sleepover Club. Dad reckoned their silly behaviour could've have caused a major accident, with all the candles and 'nonsense'. Candle holders or no candle holders, fire was dangerous stuff and he would speak to Mum about it.

Yes, in case you hadn't guessed, it was not witches or ghouls that had given us the fright of our lives. It was my dear sister and her silly friend. And if Molly and Jilly thought they'd win by scaring us with ghostly tricks like shaking the caravan, they were wrong. Dad told them so in no uncertain terms.

Finally Dad stomped off to get on the phone to the other parents.

Whew!

But in less than half an hour the grown-ups had come to pick up their 'naughty' daughters, and everyone, including Jilly, was taken home.

Ooops.

The only one left was Frankie. Her mum and dad were out, so Dad had to let her to stay. He wasn't best pleased about that, either. 'Course, it wasn't the sleepover we'd planned, but at least, me and my best friend were together, while Molly the Monster had to share with Emma. One nil to the Sleepover Club!

Before Dad could go on any more, me and Frankie did our famous getting-ready-for-bed race (one minute two seconds!) and leapt into bed. When Dad came up to check on us we were already hiding under our duvets.

"Frankie, I'll speak to your parents tomorrow," Dad said as he snapped out the bedroom light, leaving us in total darkness.

I waited 'til he'd gone downstairs. "What do you think your mum and dad'll do?" I whispered to Frankie.

"Boil me in oil… Tear me from limb to limb…"

"No, really."

"Dunno. Pass me the sweets."

We needed some comfort after Dad's ear-wigging. So we had our own Sleepover mini-feast and told each other jokes. Here are a couple that cheered us up:

**Question:** What do you get when you mix a cross witch with ice cubes?

**Answer:** A cold spell.

**Question:** How do witches drink tea?

**Answer:** With a cup and sorcerer.

And Frankie's favourite:

### Sign at a Witches' Demo:
"We demand Sweeping Reforms!"

You know how you get the giggles after you've been in trouble? Well, we did. Big Time. We couldn't stop. I think we fell asleep laughing, just when the bedroom was beginning to get light again…

Thank goodness for Frankie.

My best friend didn't get boiled in oil, or torn limb from limb, but she got grounded. The whole gang did. No more visits, no more sleepovers, no more fun until next year. Dad said he'll see if we're grown up enough for sleepovers by then. (Huh!) Still, as Frankie pointed out, we've had that threat before. And grown-ups have got very short memories, sometimes. Have you noticed that? I think they've even forgotten it's nearly Christmas, so next year's not that long to wait.

Anyway, don't get worried. The grown-ups can't stop the Sleepover gang from having fun. 'Fun' is our middle name. And they can't stop us having a fab, fab Christmas. Frankie says we have the right to sue them if they try that.

At school, things are really coo-ell too. Mrs Weaver is letting us plan a sooper-dooper Christmas party, so our class is dead excited. We're decorating the classroom and bringing food and CDs and playing games. It's gonna be ace. Then there's the Nativity play and the Carol Service…

It was at the school Carol Service that the grown-ups started to soften. Probably the sight of their little darlings dressed as angels did it. All the mums had got those soppy smiles grown-ups always get at the school Nativity play and Carol Service. So I thought I'd make the most of it, by handing round the mince pies in my angel costume.

"Mince pie, Mrs Sidebotham?" I said sweetly.

"Thank you, Laura," smiled Fliss's mum. "That was beautiful singing, just now."

"Thank you."

"Yes. A much better sound than screaming," said Mum with a twinkle in her eye.

"Mu-um!" I groaned. "That was ages and ages ago. We haven't had a single sleepover since Hallowe'en."

The mums gave each other one of those looks that said, 'Good thing too!'.

"It's not fair!" Frankie in her angel's wings looked as if she was about to take off. "We've got rights!"

Her mum looked at her fondly. Then she spoke up. "The Sleepover Club means a lot to them. Perhaps they've learnt their lesson."

"We have," chimed in Fliss, her angel costume billowing round her. "We'll never do spells again."

"Promise," added Rosie.

"Pleeeease can we have a Christmas sleepover?" begged Lyndz, putting her hands together like she was praying. Which looked dead good with her halo and stuff. "Please, please, please?"

The mums looked at one another again. Then my mum said the magic words:

"We'll see."

And you know what that means in Adult Speak, don't you?

YAY! One nil to the Sleepover Club!

Mind you, Fliss was telling the truth when she said we wouldn't do any more spells. We were being right little goody goodies these days. But that didn't stop the spells we did on Hallowe'en from working their magic. And, messing about or not, some of them did work in a funny kind of way.

For a start, Rosie reckons things at home are more peaceful. Her brother Adam (the one with cerebral palsy) has an amazing new wheelchair, and he's practising a brilliant new wheelie routine in it for Christmas. And Rosie's mum's boyfriend has promised to paint their hall in the new year, so the place won't look so much of a bomb site. Of course, Rosie's dad isn't back with her mum, but, as I reminded her, spells are only spells. Not miracles.

Lyndz hasn't got her horse yet but Frankie's giving her one from her miniature collection for Christmas, so in a way Lyndz will get her wish. (And don't tell Frankie, but I bought her a cute little china puppy for Christmas. It cost a whole week's pocket money, but I reckon my best friend is worth it.)

Oh, you want to know about Fliss, too? Well, she hasn't seen fairies at the bottom of her garden yet, but (secretly) I think she's still looking. Fliss got it the worst of all of us, really. Her mum took the spell-making stuff deadly seriously and it didn't matter how much Fliss explained it was 'just fun', Mrs Sidebotham was furious. She said witchcraft was 'dangerous mischief' and she docked Fliss's pocket money. Mind you, Fliss gets so much pocket money, that only makes her in the same boat as all of us now.

I s'pose the spell stuff did get a teeny weeny

bit out of hand… But like I told you before, the Sleepover gang is mega good at Pretend. So good that, believe it or not, my Love Potion did work some kind of magic.

It happened like this…

On the day of Molly's swimming gala, Mum made me go with her to cheer Molly on. "It's time you buried the hatchet and gave you sister some support," she said firmly.

True enough, my sneaky sister could do with some help. Molly has been what my mum calls 'spreading herself thin' lately. She's been going to Chess Club one week and swimming the next, so now her swimming speed's rubbish. Still, with her own school pool she doesn't have to rely on summer openings at the public baths like we do at our school. So Molly can practise in the new year to get back up to her 'Olympic Standard' (ha, ha).

At the pool, I did my best to cheer her on, for Mum's sake. I shouted and waved and whistled, like a real fan. I've had plenty of practice at that when I go to Leicester City football matches. So I got into the act. But the funny thing was, as I got into shouting and clapping like mad, I really began to feel it.

Suddenly I wanted Molly to swim well. I wanted her to beat the others and I wanted her to win like mad.

"Come on, Molly!" I shouted. "WIN! WIN! WIN!"

She didn't win of course. But when she came fifth… guess who was waiting on the sidelines to comfort her?

Robin Hughes!

Yes, the Chess Wiz himself actually praised Molly's effort, and what's more, Molly seemed to like it. (Heh, heh, maybe I am a witch after all…)

So, the Sleepover Club actually got a boy interested in Molly the Monster. Will wonders never cease? It only goes to prove, what I've said before… The Sleepover Club can do anything!

Wonder what we'll do next?

Think I'll just take a look in my crystal ball…

# Top Sleepover TIPS

If you thought our caravan sleepover was **coo-el**, here's how to have your own **spooky** Halloween party...

# Fliss's Witchy Fashion Tips

Pink's my fave colour, but if
you want to look super witchy,
why don't you...

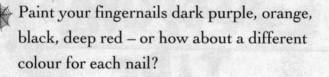

 Paint your fingernails dark purple, orange,
black, deep red – or how about a different
colour for each nail?

 Wear black everything! Or match your
clothes to your nails.

Use clashing eye shadow – what about
green and purple together?

 Create a scary hairstyle by back-combing your
hair and making it stick up on end (this works
best if you haven't washed your hair that day).

# Rosie and Lyndz's Spooky Snacks

## Bonfire Bananas

## You will need:
- Bananas
- Chocolate buttons
- Tin foil
- A knife
- Oven gloves

**1** Slit a banana lengthwise, through the skin and into the flesh with a knife.

**2** Get a handful of chocolate buttons and push them into the slit you have made.

**3** Wrap the banana in tin foil and push into the embers of the bonfire. (Get an adult to do this.)

**4** Remove after twenty minutes (with oven gloves!) and unwrap the foil.

**5** Peel the skin off for a yummy banana and chocolate suprise!

# Frankie and Kenny's Gruesome Games

## Pumpkin Carving

### You will need (per person):

- One pumpkin
- One spoon
- One sharp knife
- One night-light

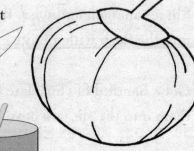

1. Carefully cut the top off your pumpkin and carve the insides out using a spoon.

2. Each person carves a scary Halloween face into their pumpkin skin.

**③** Put a lit night-light in each pumpkin and turn out the lights.

**④** When you've finished, put the pumpkins out in the garden and watch them glow.

**⑤** The scariest carving wins.

## No sharp knives allowed?

🕸 Get a black pen and draw a scary face on your pumpkin.

🕸 Blow up some orange balloons and draw scary faces on them. You can then use them to decorate the room or front door.

# Apple Bobbing

## You will need:

- One washing-up bowl or bucket
- One apple for each person

## Here's how to play:

(1) Fill the bowl/bucket with water.

(2) Float the apples in the water.

(3) Each person must remove an apple from the water using only their mouth. No hands allowed!

(4) The person with the most apples wins.

# Wrap the Mummy

## You will need:

- Three rolls of toilet tissue per team

## Here's how to play:

1. Divide into two teams.

2. Each team picks one person to be the "mummy".

3. Using the toilet paper, each team must wrap their mummy until they're completely covered.

4. The team who wraps their mummy the quickest is the winner!

# Spooky Stories

 Turn the lights down low.

② Sit in a circle.

③ One person starts the spooky story;
after a minute the person on the
speaker's left carries on the story.
With each new person the story
should get scarier and scarier...

Hope you have a spook-tastic
time! Heh, heh, heh...

Kenny x

**You** are invited to join Frankie, Lyndz, Rosie, Kenny and me for our next sleepover in...

The SleePover Club

**Be My Valentine**

There's a guy in my class I reeeeally like. But should I send him a Valentine's card? My friends just think I'm being silly, but maybe you can help...

Are you in the mood for lurve?

Come along and

**Join the club!**

From *Fliss* ✗

**p.s.** Turn the page for a sneak preview...

Hello! It's me, Fliss. Felicity Diana Sidebotham, to be precise. How are you? Glad to hear it. I'm fine too – even after the traumatic few weeks I've just had! Sometimes if Mum's had a hard day, or if my little brother Callum's playing up, she says her nerves are "jangled" – and now I think I know what she means! Mine have been doing a lot of jangling too lately, with all the Valentine goings-on. Thank goodness *that*'s all over with for another year!

I love the idea of Valentine's Day though, don't you? I think it's *soooo* romantic. I can't wait till I'm a bit older and start getting bunches of flowers and boxes of chocolates and soppy cards through the post. Kenny sort of scoffs at me about it and says I've been reading too many fairy tales, but I just think there's something wonderful about the idea of being swept off your feet by a handsome prince, or knight in armour, or… you know what I mean. My mum's exactly the same. If Andy, my mum's boyfriend, ever *dared* forget about Valentine's Day, there would be big trouble in our house!!

Anyway, as I'm still pretty young, there hasn't been much romance for me on Valentine's Days so far. Crispin Potter once made a card for me when we were in the Infants, but I don't think that counts, do you? He's got horrible freckles anyway and is one of those boys who runs round shouting and pushing people all the time now. I think I preferred him when he was five, to be honest…

This year though, love seemed to be well and truly in the air at school. Usually we make a big fuss of seasonal things at school – like we always make calendars and Christmas cards in December, and we do stuff for Easter and Halloween, but we've never really done anything for Valentine's Day before. Until this year, when even the Sleepover Club found itself getting caught up with it!

It all started at the beginning of February, when Mrs Weaver – that's our teacher – walked into the classroom with a big, red, heart-shaped box which she plonked on her desk.

"Can anyone guess what this is for?" she asked us. Everyone was staring at it, wondering what was coming next.

Frankie's arm shot up. "You're gonna tell us how much you love us, Mrs Weaver?" she suggested.

Mrs Weaver's eyes twinkled a bit. I think she's got a soft spot for Frankie, you know.

"No... You're on the right lines, though," she said. "Anyone else? Think what month we're into now."

"February..." everyone muttered to themselves – and then you could almost hear twenty-eight brains ticking over. "Valentine's Day!" we all said, practically at the same time.

"Very good!" she said, writing it up on the board. "And what happens on Valentine's Day?"

"Ugh, lots of horrible mushy stuff," said Crispin Potter, pulling a face. Typical! I felt myself going red and deliberately didn't look at him – I didn't want him to remember the "horrible mushy" card he'd made for me four years ago!!

"People fall in love," simpered Emily Berryman, lowering her eyelashes in this coy way. UGH!! Her and her yucky mate Emma Hughes are our big rivals. The M&Ms, we call them. And don't be fooled by what Emily just said either – there's nothing nice about those two. They're EVIL!!

"Yes, people might fall in love, but what about people who already love each other?" Mrs Weaver asked. "What do they do?"

I put my hand up.

"Yes, Felicity?"

"They send each other big cards and presents and go out for romantic dinners," I said, feeling important.

"Yes, if you're lucky!" Mrs Weaver said.

"Does your husband take you out for romantic dinners, Miss?" Simon Graham shouted out from the back of the classroom.

Mrs Weaver laughed. She seemed in a very good mood this morning – sometimes she gets a bit narky if people ask personal things like that. "Well, I'm crossing my fingers, Simon," she told him. "Let's hope so, eh!"

Then she picked up the heart-shaped box. "As it's Valentine's Day this month, every class in the school is going to have one of these post-boxes in the classroom. So if there's anyone in the school you like – send them a Valentine! You don't have to put your name on your card or note – you can send a secret one, if you'd rather. We're going to have a Valentine Disco in a fortnight, so you can even ask someone to be your date for the evening!"

"Yeeeuck!!" said one of the boys. "I'm not sending any!"

"What if you hate all the boys in the world?" Kenny said, pulling a face at Stuart Brown, this boy she'd just fallen out with in the playground. "Can you send hate mail?"

"Of course you can't, Laura," said Mrs

Weaver. (Laura is Kenny's real name if you didn't know – Laura McKenzie. But don't call her that if you value your life!) "But you could send a friendship note to one of your friends instead."

"Hmmmphh," said Kenny, still not very impressed with the idea.

"She doesn't have any friends," said Stuart Brown, trying to flick a paper-clip at her.

"I've got more than you!" she shot back, chucking a pen-lid at him. "Stuart No-Mates!"

"Well, let's see how many cards you two get – then we'll all know, won't we?" Mrs Weaver said.

Very crafty! Goad Kenny into a competition, and you know she'll throw everything into it to win! Kenny shot us all meaningful looks which said, plain as anything, that we'd all better send her a friendship note or our lives wouldn't be worth living!

I had a plan of my own, anyway. There's this boy in our class that I really *reeeeally* like. You might think it sounds a bit daft, but I want to marry him when we're grown up. I've got it all worked out! Ryan Scott, his name is. He's dead nice and well-mannered and has nice clothes. I think he likes me, too. The others tease me about it sometimes but I reckon they're just jealous. Maybe if I sent him a card, he might ask me to the Valentine Disco...

**To be continued...**

**You** are invited to join
Lyndz, Kenny, Fliss,
Rosie and me for our first
Sleepover Club story in...

Want to know how we all became
friends, had our first sleepover and
formed the Best Club in the World Ever!

Come on! What are **you** waiting for?
**Join the club!**

From

Frankie x

**YOU** are invited to join Frankie, Fliss, Kenny, Rosie and me for our next sleepover in...

TV  Stars!

When Fliss persuaded us to come to her audition, we all got into the acting groove! Time to climb our way up the celeb ladder!

Are **you** set for stardom? Come along and join the club!

From

*Lyndz* ✗

**You** are invited to join Frankie, Lyndz, Fliss, Kenny and me for our next sleepover in...

The Sleepover Club

# Dance-Off!

The Sleepover Babes are on a mission to win the school dance competition - no way are we letting our enemies, the M&Ms, dance all over us!

Have **you** got some funky moves? Come along and join the club!

From

Rosie x

# YOU

are invited to join Frankie, Lyndz, Fliss, Rosie and me on our next crazy adventure in...

# The SleePover Club

# Hit the Beach!

I L.O.V.E. sports and am soooo excited about our school trip. A week away from home with my best friends by the seaside - time to catch some waves!

Are **you** up for some fun in the sun? Grab your shades and join the club!

From

Kenny x